FEATURING DR. STRANGE, ANT-MAN AND CAPTAIN AMERICA

THOR

FEATURING DR. STRANGE, ANT-MAN AND CAPTAIN AMERICA

Writers: *Paul Tobin, Fred Van Lente, Louise Simonson Scott Gray & Roger Langridge*
Pencilers: *Jacopo Campagni, Matteo Lolli, Rodney Buchemi & Craig Rousseau*
Inkers: *Norman Lee, Christian Vecchia, Rodney Buchemi & Craig Rousseau*
Colorists: *Guru eFx & Chris Sotomayor*
Letterer: *Dave Sharpe*
Cover Art: *Roger Cruz & Wil Quintana; Clayton Henry & Guru eFx; and Salva Espin, Karl Kesel & Pete Pantazis*
Assistant Editor: *Jordan D. White*
Consulting Editors: *Mark Paniccia & Ralph Macchio*
Editor: *Nathan Cosby*

Collection Editor: *Jennifer Grünwald*
Editorial Assistant: *Alex Starbuck*
Assistant Editors: *Cory Levine & John Denning*
Editor, Special Projects: *Mark D. Beazley*
Senior Editor, Special Projects: *Jeff Youngquist*
Senior Vice President of Sales: *David Gabriel*

Editor in Chief: *Joe Quesada*
Publisher: *Dan Buckley*
Executive Producer: *Alan Fine*

#5

I travel a lot. Especially in the mornings.
As Earth's Sorcerer Supreme, as the Master of the Mystic Arts, as Dr. Strange, it's my task to make sure all is right in the magical realms.
First I check if the Mindless Ones are still behaving.
Then it's always a good idea to make sure that Umar the Unrelenting is still dormant. Or at least not turning her energies to Earth.
And I need to make sure that Nisilette the Unimaginable is still not being imagined.
After a few other tasks, I always like to end by making sure the fabric of reality is still tightly woven, with no tears or loose threads or--

Uh-oh.
Reality. Shredded. Holes everywhere.
It's been--eaten? What could have--oh. Of course. There's only one creature that eats reality like this.
It would be foolish to attempt this without backup. But who would be best? The Ancient One is too frail for--
--ah! Yes. I've got it. I know just the man. He's perfectly suited for this task, considering his unique and amazing abilities. More importantly, he's confident.
Now...
A Very Strange Day
Paul Tobin--Writer Jacopo Camagni--Penciler
Norman Lee--Inker Guru eFx--Colorists Cruz & Quintana--Cover
Anthony Dial--Production Mark Paniccia & Ralph Macchio--Consulting
Nathan Cosby--Editor Joe Quesada--Editor In Chief Dan Buckley--Publisher

...to find him.
MANHATTAN...
Nothing like a good morning workout.
Other guys go jogging. I web-sling across town. Talk to pigeons.
Check to make sure nobody's robbing the banks and that the Vulture's not flying across Manhattan, creating all sorts of havoc.

No purse-snatchers, car thieves, muggers? Good.
No giant rampaging robots that are way out of my league? Even better.
So why's my Spidey-sense going off?
KKKKSSHAAASHHH
Oh.
That.
Spider-Man?! How did you know?
How did I know? Easy, Vulture, I always study before a test. But, uhh, exactly what do I know?
Stop him! Stop the Vulture! He's stealing the Gnarian Orb!

What's the Gnarly Orb?
Something for a very important client. And it's Gnarian.

It does all sorts of neat things. Like, it smashes spiders. See?
CHOKK
Unnhh! Geez! I woulda taken your word for it!

Gotcha!
Good thing I've been webbing pigeons for practice.
You're about to wish you'd been practicing escapes. I've had enough of--

Huh?!! I'm-- stuck!!
How are you doing this?!!

I'm not doing it. I'm not even sure-- oh. Hey. You're ummm-- there you are.
What is going on?!!

It's magic.
Whoa! Where'd you--
I need your help, Spider-Man.
Uhh, excuse me, but I'm kinda fighting the Vulture right now.
No problem-- I'll just teleport his stolen property to the proper owner, and the Vulture to a police station.
Hey! Hey! HEY!
Dang, that's kinda handy.
Not something I often have a chance to do. Most of my own foes aren't quite right for police stations.
Where are you poking your head in from?
A reality nexus. Which is why I need your help. Something's wrong. Can I depend on you?
Depend on me for what?
I'll show you.
What?!! Uh, okay. I think.
We're at a nexus point for millions of realities, and the problem is this. The fabric of reality.
It's all torn up. Eaten. That's bad, right?
Yes. Very.

The way that we can solve this--
So, I thought I'd introduce myself. I'm Spider-Man.
Yes, of course I know that. Now, as I was saying--
--oh.
I see. My apologies.
I get so caught up in the mystical realms that I forget not everyone knows about them.
I'm Dr. Strange. Earth's Sorcerer Supreme.
We have a Sorcerer Supreme? I mean, I think that pepperoni is considered Earth's Most Favorite Pizza, but Earth having a Sorcerer Supreme is news to me.
My fault. I should have anticipated your questions about me, and why you should trust me. Here. Come this way.
Okay. Sure. Great. To where?
The easiest way to introduce myself is to go below reality. To the past.
The, uh, past?
Yes. This was me, Stephen Strange, before I began to study magic.
I was a neurosurgeon. Probably the best.

But whatever brilliance I possessed, I had twice that much arrogance.
I had to have everything my way. Important friends. Houses. Cars. Everything.
Doc, it doesn't sound, or look, like you were a very nice guy.
No. Luckily, my out-of-control life took its toll on me.
My mental state broke down, and there was a car accident.
Wait, a lucky car accident?
In the end, yes. My hands were damaged. My abilities as a neurosurgeon, my very life, were shattered. But eventually it served as a wake-up call. Of course at first I spiraled into despondency. Madness.
Jason Wong, a friend from my college days, tried to help me restore my mental health. Took me to a host of doctors. Nobody could help.
Finally, in desperation, he brought me to the Himalayas in search of a man called the Ancient One.
Over the course of several months, I learned mental exercises that helped me restore my balance.
The exercises gave me perspective. Stability.
To my surprise, the Ancient One eventually revealed that he'd been teaching me rudimentary magic, and that I was a natural student.

The Ancient One was then Earth's Sorcerer Supreme, charged with safeguarding Earth from all magical threats.
But he was tired. Unbelievably old. He wanted to pass on the mantle.
And so Jason and I stayed on in that timeless place, and I began training.
It took years. *Long* years. But now I am, more or less, *ready* for the task.
More or less? *That* sounds encouraging.
Learning the mystic arts is like learning a river's current. By the time you understand it, the pathways *change;* water is flowing in other directions.
You have to learn to guide the water yourself. *Become* the water. *Become* the current. Become *the river.*
Now you're sounding all *mystic.*
Well, *yes.*
I've set up this house in Greenwich Village and I operate from here.
Wait--I *know* this street. Bleecker Street. This house has *never* been here *before.*
It's normally magically shielded from view. Certain people, such as you from now on, are permitted to see it.

I live here with my friends, Jason Wong and the Ancient One, who still has much to teach me. At the same time, I've been teaching him about the world.
Do you really just call him the Ancient One?
Yes. He likes it. Unfortunately, he's too frail for interdimensional travel, or else I would have gone to him for help with this problem.
Instead, I've come to you for your unique abilities.
I believe that brings us up to date. We should probably be on our way.
Yeah--if we're in such a big hurry, why the grand tour of your past?
It actually only took us one second.
A second? Wait, one second? How does--oh, sure. Yeah. I get it. Magic.
Right. Magic. Now, the creature that ate the--
We're under attack.
Yikes!
Don't get bitten! Those fangs are poisonous!
Don't get bitten? Great advice! Thanks!

Okay, if you're going to bite, then I'm going to pull hair.
Urggghh?!
THMMMRP
THOOOM
Unnnfff!
Okay-- what were those?
Zakimiya young. I'm banishing them.
Zaki-what's that? Come again?
Zakimiya. Newborn. They're what's been eating holes in the fabric of reality. Somewhere out there in the magical realms, an adult zakimiya is spawning.
Frankly, it's amazingly rare. Such things only happen once every, oh, fifty million years.
I'm very excited by this. We might actually see an adult zakimiya.
Yeah, we should both get party hats. Listen, isn't this really bad?
Yes, but I'm trying to look on the bright side. I have to.

Magic and sorcery are largely about confidence. If I let myself get too disheartened or depressed, well then--
Got it. The rabbit doesn't come out of the hat.
Right. Hold still for a second.
ZAPPT
Hey! What'd you do?!!
We need to fix these holes in reality. I just temporarily bumped up some of your powers. Linked them to a magical base.
Now all these problem areas will trigger your danger sense. They are dangerous, after all.
How do you know about my Spidey-sense?
Sorcerer Supreme side benefit. We just know things. Now, if you would, web this problem area shut.
Huh, you mean, just with my webbing?
Yes.
There. See? I've ramped up your webbing, too. It works on a magical basis, for now.
Your webbing will protect the hole while it naturally heals.
THWIP!
Great, so I'm Spidey 2.0. What's next?
We follow the adult zakimiya's trail. It will be moving through different realities, spawning as it travels, letting its offspring chow down on reality.
And when we catch up to the adult, what then?

Oh, I have no idea. We're certainly no match for it.
Man, I'm glad you're able to keep your confidence up. Mine's a little wobbly.
Now where are we?
A reality known as Settleshine.
Duck for a moment.
KSSSSSTT!
Yikes!
No worries. I've got it.
Problem solved. Could you seal that hole up?
Yeah--I saw it. In fact, I sensed it.
Well, that's why I needed you along. I couldn't do this alone. There will be lots of holes and without the aid of your senses I'd almost certainly miss some.
HSSSTT!
We have to keep moving in order to catch the zakimiya.
Sure. I've been specifically training for marathon runs through realities, so this works fine.
Where to now?

This reality is called Oripp. We'll meet resistance here.
Really? Wouldn't have noticed.
Is this what being the Sorcerer Supreme is all about? Fighting cavemen?
I normally try to avoid fights of any kind. But I can handle these guys. You just keep sealing those holes.
SHHHHWOOOOOMM
Whoa! What was that?
Winds of Watoomb.
Well, they're neat.

THE BOODLEFIN REALITY...
What are you doing?
Signing a peace accord. A dual pact allowing inter-reality travel rights.
Cool.

THE REALITY OF NEM...
There's holes all over!
Hurry!

THE VERE ACTUALITY...
There's nothing here.
No. This is where Nisilette the Unimaginable would be, if she were imagined.
Who?
Never mind. Don't think of her.
THE SALA CONTINUUM...
So, if these creatures are all young zakimiya, why do they look so different?
Their looks depend on the reality where they were born. But you can always tell a zakimiya by the tusks.
They use them to rip and gouge reality before they eat it.
By Gnarian Eye and Cellan Tooth, I call upon the Crimson Bands of Cyttorak.
Did you need to speak like that in order to cast the spell?
Not really. I just find it more dramatic that way. It helps my confidence, and confidence in spell-casting is--
Yeah, you told me.
THE TTQFOLN REALITY...
Spider-Man, could I borrow some change? I sense 68 cents on you.
Umm. Okay. Why?
I'm bartering for safe passage through this reality.
For 68 cents? Guess the exchange rate must be pretty good.

Oh, it's not so much the monetary value. Think of it. From their viewpoint we gave them artifacts from an entirely different reality.
What would you do for such a gift?
Yeah. I see your point.
THE BABOLYA REALITY DRIFT...
It's close.
Yeah. I feel-- something.
These enhanced senses make it feel like an earthquake. What is it?
The zakimiya.
Ooh ho. Mortals? Here? Hmmmmm.
How would you like to be disposed of?

Beautiful?
You didn't tell me it was--
That's not actually the word I was going to use.
Such *magnificent* power. It could destroy us at *whim.*
SNAP SNAP SNAP
Oh goodie. That's *another thing* you *could* have mentioned.
But, you have a *plan,* right? Right? Hello? *Right?*
Yes. I *do* have a plan. Just now thought of one.
Start capturing all the little ones.
Huh? *All* of them? *How?*
I'm lending you some power.

Now you'll be able to shoot the *Crimson Webs of Cyttorak,* a variant of another spell.
Neat!
There. *Snare them.* As many as you can. And do it as *haughtily* and *arrogantly* as possible.
Huh?
Trust me. *Do it.*
Okay. Can do. I guess.
You there! Gnats. I ENSNARE you. Though you are all but as ANTS to me, I give you, umm, the SCINTILLATING BOON of my PRESENCE.
Perfect. Keep it up.
And now for *my* part.
Hmmm, this is rather *fun.*

Zakimiya!
Yes?
I have come to battle you.
How amusing. So be it.
Here's a little taste of the Flames of Faltine, which I've ramped up further with the Seven Suns of Cinnibus.
Yes. Yes. Faltine. Cinnibus. I know of them. Fine creatures, they are.
Let's see if you can endure a few Celian Fangs!
Oh, little speck. I can actually feel your powers. Hmmm. Yes. I am impressed.
But bored. I believe I will turn you to dust.
Turn me to dust? Oh now, that wouldn't be too smart. You would anger my master.
Your master?
Yes. The entity known as Spider-Man.

You three. CEASE. And don't... ha ha...SNIVEL in my AUGUST PRESENCE.
Oh man. This kinda rocks.
YOU. The TREMBLING ONE. Why are you not THANKING me for TAKING NOTICE of your PITIFUL EXISTENCE?
Sssst! Doc! How'm I doing?
Fine. Keep hamming it up.
Spider-Man? I know of no such entity.
Of course not. He is one of the Hidden. And yet, so powerful that my own spells have been learned in a single hour of his tutelage.
Hmmm. A Hidden One?
How DARE you awaken ME, the completely awesomely cool SPIDER-MAN, from my SLUMBER OF EONS.
I am TEMPTED to release more than this MERE MOTE of my TRUE POWER!
Hmmmm.

A Hidden One.
And I have angered him?
Such as he experiences emotion. Yes.
Hmmm.
What can I do?
Hmmm, what can be done?
What would you suggest?
Oh, such a little thing. Instruct your children to feed on something other than the fabric of reality, and I believe the Spider-Man would be placated.
Hmmm. I suppose they could eat the hearts of black holes.
Fine. It is so decided. You may leave.

Thank you, disciple of the Hidden One. You are quite kind.
Yeah. That's so true.
A merest SHRUG from I, the one for whom a THOUSAND GALAXIES have-- huh?
They all disappeared?
What happened?
Thanks to your acting, we just won on a complete bluff. You'd make a good magician, you know. Sorcery's all in the confidence.
Then why am I so sweaty?
You are? I could cast a spell that would completely neutralize your sweat glands and--
No, ahhh, no, not necessary.
Hey. We're back on Earth. And that's your house, right?
Yes. And now, since I bullied you into helping me, I'd like to pay you a little something.

Huh? No! I can't take money for saving the world. No way!
We actually saved the multi-verse. But, really, take this.
What's this? Coins?
The equivalent of 68 cents. But in Ttqfolnian money, from another reality.
Whoa! Neat. You're right. It really is kind of amazing that--
Huh? Where'd you go?
Well, I should have guessed a magician would pull a disappearing act.
Ahh, you're back. How was your day, Stephen?
Amazing, Wong.
Quite amazing.
END.

#6

HERE COMES ANT-MAN! THE MAN WITH TWO SUPER POWERS!
WHO is he? HOW did he get both the ability to shrink to less than an inch tall--and speak directly to ants? WHY does he choose to use those abilities to aid all mankind?
SHUT UP!!! DON'T ANSWER!!! THOSE ARE RHETORICAL QUESTIONS!!! YOUR ANSWERS COULDN'T POSSIBLY BE AS AWESOME AS THE REAL ONES! SO WHAT ARE YOU WAITING FOR? TURN THE PAGE!!!
THE ANTHILL... AND THE APOCALYPSE!
Written by Fred Van Lente Penciled by Matteo Lolli
Inked by Christian Vecchia Colored by Guru eFX
Lettered by Dave Sharpe Cover by Henry & Guru Production: Taylor Esposito
Consulting: Mark Paniccia & Ralph Macchio Editor: Nathan Cosby
Editor in Chief: Joe Quesada Publisher: Dan Buckley

AAAAAGHHH! ANTS!
Mommy! Mommy! Save us!!
Honey! There's ants in my under-pants!
Oh, no! Now I have to call the exterminator to spray poison on my kids, food and pets!
Not anymore!
Not with the new Pym Pest Persuader™ (patent pending)!
After years of study, the brilliant Henry Pym has developed a means to communicate directly with ants through their antennae!
Ants! Leave this house!
There is nothing for you here!
Leave this house alone!

Dear! Call off the movers! We're not leaving-- the ants are!
YAAAAY!!
No poison. No mess. It's good for people. It's good for ants. And, best of all...
TONY
...it's good for America!
So what do you think, guys?
Pretty cool, huh?
KLIK!
As you can see, I have the prototype Persuader here, and I'm ready to begin mass manufacture immediately...
...that is, if you, uh, um...
...like it...
VAN DYNE TECH
Next.

Better luck next time, Dr. Pym.
Next time? Yeah...what is this?
The twelfth grant application of mine they've shot down?
Aw, c'mon. You know how the song goes.
"Just what makes that little ole ant / Think he can move that rubber tree plant?"
"Anyone knows an ant can't / Move a rubber tree plant!"
Heh. Right.
"But he's got high hopes..."
VAN D
'Sides... I thought the Pest Persuader was pretty neat.
Thanks... Janet, yeah? You're Mr. Van Dyne's daughter.
I am, but no need to hold that against me, Doc.
Hank. I won't! I appreciate the cheering up.
VAN DYNE TECH
"I just wish everybody was as understanding as you..."
PYM!!! OPEN UP, PYM!!
BANG
BANG
BANG

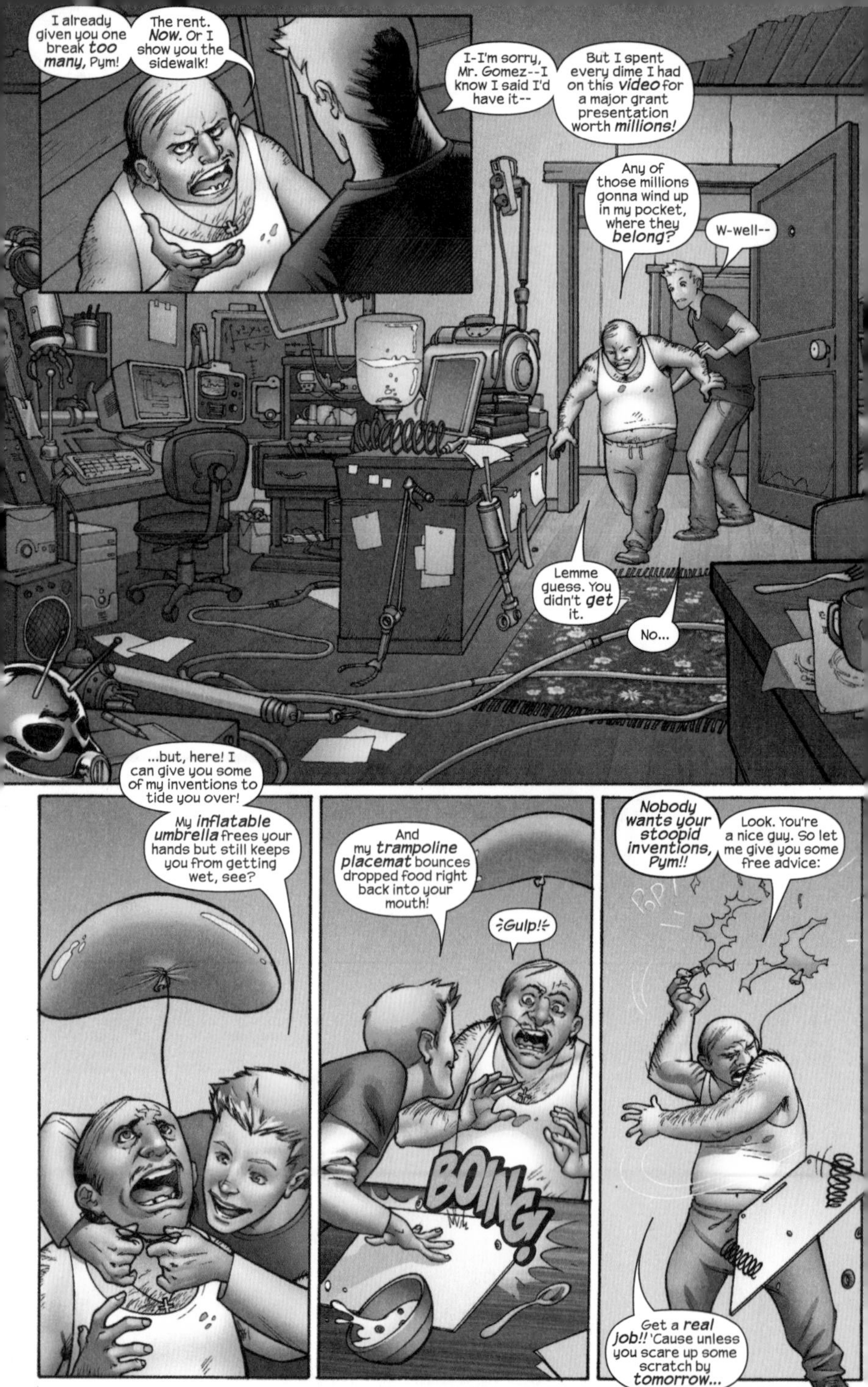
I already given you one break too many, Pym!
The rent. Now. Or I show you the sidewalk!
I-I'm sorry, Mr. Gomez--I know I said I'd have it--
But I spent every dime I had on this video for a major grant presentation worth millions!
Any of those millions gonna wind up in my pocket, where they belong?
W-well--
Lemme guess. You didn't get it.
No...
...but, here! I can give you some of my inventions to tide you over!
My inflatable umbrella frees your hands but still keeps you from getting wet, see?
And my trampoline placemat bounces dropped food right back into your mouth!
Gulp!
BOING!
Nobody wants your stoopid inventions, Pym!!
Look. You're a nice guy. So let me give you some free advice:
Get a real job!! 'Cause unless you scare up some scratch by tomorrow...

...I gotta give you the *boot!* No foolin'!
SLAM!
I hate to admit it...but he's right!

Ever since I was a kid it was my dream to be a famous inventor--
--but why should I keep bashing my head against a wall that *won't fall down?*

First thing tomorrow I'm gonna start acting like a *grown-up!* I'll go out and find myself some steady work.
YAWN...!
It may not be what I *wanted* out of life--but it *will* be a nice change of pace to know I'll be able to pay my bills for once...
Help Wanted

Z
Z
Hank! Psst... Hank!

HANK! WAKE UP!
We really need your help!
Wha--?!
I said I'd get you the rent tomorrow, Mr. Gomez...

Mister...?
Hey...
Who's there?

We're over here!
In...the Persuader?

Am I still asleep...?
We know how you're trying to make your fellow Big Ones stop using poison on us, Hank!

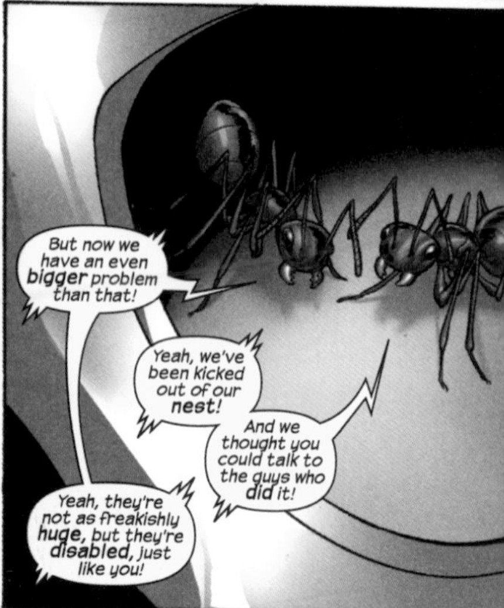
But now we have an even bigger problem than that!
Yeah, we've been kicked out of our nest!
And we thought you could talk to the guys who did it!
Yeah, they're not as freakishly huge, but they're disabled, just like you!

Dude. Don't say "disabled."
What? What should I call him, then?
The politically correct term is "physically challenged."

How am I physically challenged?
You know... you're missing four legs!
How you manage to soldier on under such hardship is a testament to the human spirit! Seriously!
We think so, and we're not even human!
C'mon, we'll show you our hill! It's outside!

Dreaming.
I've got to be dreaming.
It's the only explanation.
Our colony's dug our anthill right over there for generations!
Yeah! Almost three weeks, now! But look!

Yeah, I see what you *mean.*
There's something *buried* here.
Almost seems like a...
Whoa.
Red alert!
Perimeter security breach!
BWOOP! BWOOP! BWOOP!
Initiate "de-big-i-fication!"
VWOO WOO WOO WOO WOO WOO
Now I *pray* I'm dreaming!

Um...
...this isn't really turning out how we planned.
Should we run?
Do aphids taste like sweet, sweet candy?

Yow!
Leggo!
Resistance is futile, Earth creatures!!

Sorry we dragged you into this, Hank!
But...what is this, exactly? Are we being invaded by aliens from outer space?

Not outer space, witless Earthman!
Inner space! The Microverse teeming in the gaps between this world's molecules!
A kingdom too tiny to contain my ambitions--
I...
PSYCHO-MAN!!

Did you honestly think you--one man--could expose my secret invasion plans to the world?
Actually... no. No, I didn't.
SILENCE!!! YOUR LIES NAUSEATE ME!
Our home planet in the Microverse has become over-populated!
So I used my "Big-i-fication Ray" to expand our invasion force into this world!
I grew us as far as our insectoid exoskeletons would allow...lest they become too large and crush our own bodies!
After commandeering this Earth hive as my hidden base, my men have concealed EMOTICON® Projectors throughout the city!
Soon--as I shall demonstrate on my Command Box--
They will project waves of depression across the globe that will put all of mankind into an inexplicable funk!
And then--when I adjust the EMOTICONS® to send out joy instead of sadness, just as I reveal myself to humanity--
--in their gratitude, gullible Earth fools will unanimously elect me Supreme Perfect Leader of Everything!
(At least, that's how I came to power in the Microverse...)

There! Now that you know my master plan in laborious detail, I shall throw you into my cells--
--where the knowledge you can do nothing to stop me may torture your every waking moment! HA HA HA HA HA!!
The Queen and her courtiers! Thank goodness! We feared you were lost when the aliens attacked!
Your Majesty-- though we succeeded in locating the Big One hero Henry Pym, as you can see...
Fear not, Kjjskkk XI and Qqqlllllsssskkk XVII. We know you did the best you could, and we are pleased.
You had no way of knowing the invaders' technology could get the better of even The Great and Mighty Pym.
I don't believe it! This stinks!
My whole life I've been trying to be somebody-- but every door I knock on gets slammed in my face!
Now I find out I'm a hero to you ants--but so what? At the time you need me most, I'm a zero to you, too!
Don't sweat it, Hank!
Yeah, we know you tried your best!
That's just it! I'm always trying my best...

...and it's never good enough!
SHRUNCH!
DUDE!!
WHAMMMO!
...we can blow this alien pop stand!
Freedom! Terrible, terrible freedom!
Wow! I guess... when Psycho-Man "de-big-i-fied" me...
...he just compacted my density! So even though I'm an inch tall, I retain my normal-size strength!
So... he's gained the proportionate strength, speed and agility...
That means...
...of a human? Am I supposed to be impressed?
Hold up, guys! The guards are just ahead!
How can you tell? Are your "Human-Senses" tingling?
Sssssshh!!!
Feels like...
...these uniforms work like armor too... Hmmm...

AND SO...
C'mon, guys! That psycho Psycho-Man's command center is this way!
You lead, we'll follow, Hank!
FIZAK
Incredible! Even accounting for the armor, their ray blasts aren't affecting me at all!
Shrunk down like this, my greater density must make me unusually resistant to injury...
...not to mention making me equally good at dishing it out!
POW!
Say--I wonder what those controls on my belt do?
But I have no time to tinker! Gotta stay focused!
Everything is going exactly as I planned--as usual!

Waves of existential ennui are crippling the city!
I don't see the point in doin' this no more!
Me neither! Garbage is just gonna start pilin' up again tomorrow! Sniff!
All Earth creatures are affected--from all walks of life!
Alert the Microverse! Prepare our brethren for the total colonization of Earth! Ha ha ha ha!!
Janet!
No!!

You leave her alone!
C'mon, guys! We gotta stop him!
With pleasure, Hank!
What? What is the meaning of this?
NO ONE WILL STOP ME FROM BUMMING OUT THIS PLANET!!
...when the Control BOX casts a shadow of doubt over his psyche!
WWAAAAAA!
Let's see if this Earth spy is so sure of himself...
Wait...
...what am I doing? I'm no super hero!
I've been a total screw-up my whole life! And I'm supposed to save Earth? Yeah, right!
That's never gonna happen! I should just quit while I'm ahead!

Uh-oh. He's at it again.
We gotta buck up his spirits, gang!
A-one-and-a-two-and-a...
"Just what makes that little ole ant / Think he'll move that rubber tree plant?"
"Anyone knows an ant can't / Move a rubber tree plant!"
"But he's got...HIIIIIGH HOPES..."
"He's got... HIIIIIIGH HOPES..."
It's true! I do have high hopes!
And that's all I've ever had! I may not be rich, or successful, or, even, um, liked...
...but I'm happy tinkering in my lab and coming up with new inventions! And there's nothing more important than that!
"So anytime you're getting' low / 'Stead of lettin' go, / Just remember that ant!"
NO!! They're thwarting me with song! I hate it when people do that!
IT'S LIKE MY INVASION OF NEXU-IV ALL OVER AGAIN!!
And I think I just figured out what these controls do!
"Whoops, there goes another rubber tree plant!!"

Each one of these suits contains its own Big-i-fication Ray!
SKRONCH!
How-- how is this possible?!?
All my research showed that's an impossible size to achieve through big-i-fication! He should be collapsing in on himself!
You go, Hank!
It's almost as if...as if his skeleton is on the inside of his body or something!!*
*:It is.--Ed.
YOU NEVER TOLD ME THIS PLANET WAS POPULATED BY GENETIC FREAKS!!
Um...that's because I'm the janitor.
YAAAAAAHH!
Eep!
A LIKELY EXCUSE!
ALL MICROVERSIANS MUST BE PREPARED TO GIVE THEIR LIVES FOR THEIR PERFECT LEADER!

I must save *myself*--for the good of the Microversian people!
I must survive to plot and scheme and regain our *honor* through revenge against this... this *Ant-Man!*
Wha--?
Ga?
GA!!
AAAAAAAAAA!!!

GAAAAAAAA!!!
SCRAPT
AAAAAAAAA!!!

The invaders are shrinking away, back to the Micro-verse! The colony is saved!
YAAAAAY, HANK!!
Thanks, guys. I literally couldn't have done it without you--and your belief in me!
And the best part of this whole deal is I got my hands on this incredible shrinking and growing technology!
Once I walk into Van Dyne Tech tomorrow with this belt...
"...my money problems will be over for good!"
VAN DYNE TECH
Back for more punishment, Hank?
You changed my whole attitude around, Janet!
I've got a feeling my luck is going to change--starting today!
How are you?
Aw, I'm all right. I was feeling really down, last night, couldn't sleep.
R-really? How come?
I'm not sure, but it could be...
Look, don't get me wrong. I love my father. I do.
But sometimes, the products he makes--the power he has--

--some-times he doesn't think through the *consequences* they have on *society!*
I mean, sometimes it seems like all Dad cares about is *profits!*
I feel like I have to tell him that sometimes, but I haven't mustered the courage yet...

What do *you* think I should do, Hank?
Hank?
Where'd you go?
Don't you have a *presentation* to give...?

BACK HOME:
Decided not to sell the belt after all, huh, Hank?
No...shrinking power is too *world-changing* to allow any human to have it--not until I've had the chance to *test* it some more, first.
The only person I can trust not to *abuse* it... is *me!*

I can keep on helping people with the power, though!
If only I could think of a good hero name to call myself...
But you guys are going to have to make room for me and my equipment in your anthill! I don't have the rent, so Mr. Gomez is gonna kick me out on the street!

What if you gave him this?
What is it?
We found it buried out in the courtyard a while ago.
We don't have any use for it, but we know you Big Ones have some strange customs!

It's filled with old silver dollars! Some miser must have buried it decades ago!
This will cover my rent-- and then some! Thanks, guys!
It's the least we could do for saving our nest, Hank!
And if you shrink down, our Queen has another surprise for you!

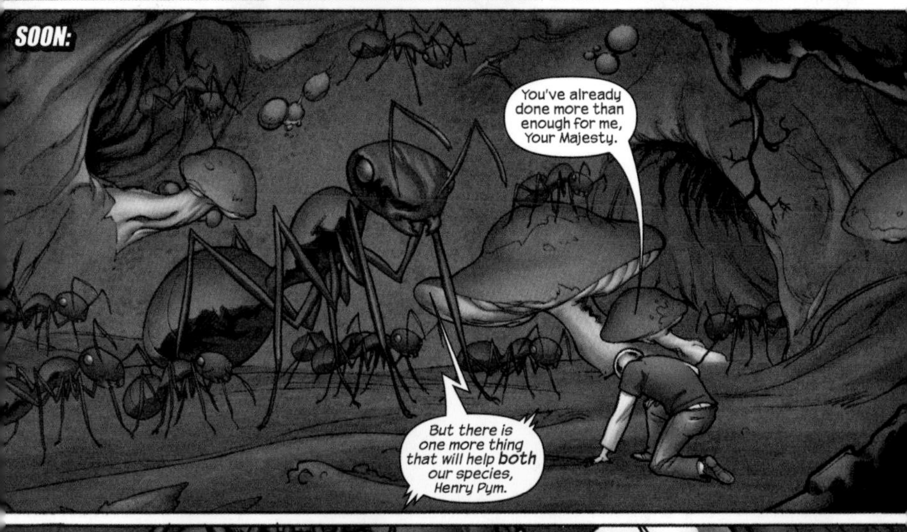
SOON:
You've already done more than enough for me, Your Majesty.
But there is one more thing that will help both our species, Henry Pym.

You would honor us by accepting the hand of our daughter, Princess Kkkrrkkkikk, in marriage!
IIII wuuuvvv yoooou, Henreee Pyyyym...
GAK!
By which I mean, uh... Thanks, Your Highness...
...but I'll just take the money...
A HERO IS BORN!

#7

WHAKK!

Cease your *thievery*, craven varlets!

The safety of all who dwell on *Earth* is Thor's charge...

THWOK!

...and those who *threaten* that safety must answer to *me!*

WHOK!

DOCTOR DONALD BLAKE POSSESSES A MAGICAL CANE THAT TURNS HIM INTO THE ASGARDIAN GOD OF THUNDER...

THE MIGHTY THOR!

LIP SERVICE

LOUISE SIMONSON WRITER RODNEY BUCHEMI ART
GURU eFX COLOR DAVE SHARPE LETTERING ESPIN, KESEL & PANTAZIS COVER
TOM VAN CISE PRODUCTION JORDAN D. WHITE ASSISTANT EDITOR RALPH MACCHIO CONSULTING

Those... thugs--! I was terrified! I'm so glad you happened by!
I too am glad, Jane!
It is ever my wish to protect the woman that I love.
That sure beat riding the subway to work!
Good-bye! And thank you! I can't wait to tell Dr. Blake what happened.
If only I could tell her that her employer already knows.
That, by the magic of the hammer Mjolnir, Thor and the doctor she so admires...
...are one.

ASGARD...
It was incredible, Donald! Robbers tried to hold up the bank but Thor stopped them!
He was... amazing!
You see how it is, Father Odin...how your son looks at the mortal woman, Jane Foster!
Despite your command, it is only a matter of time before he reveals his true nature!
If it were not forbidden that a Norse god wed a mortal, he would propose to her on the spot!
Such behavior is unseemly, Loki!
Were my son to disobey my direct order, I would punish him severely...
...as I would reward the god who cured Thor of his obsession.

NEW YORK CITY...
Curious...
What is it?
An invitation to tour the new Reptile and Amphibian House at the zoo.
The one with the special section for the most dangerous reptiles and amphibians in the world?
That's right. Afterwards, a Dutch scientist, Klaus Voorhees, will discuss his new antivenom discovery.
Oh--but a special tour would be wonderful! I'd promised to take my friend's son there for his birthday.
He loves reptiles... he's a budding herpetologist... but his mom hates snakes.
Honestly, I'm not wild about them myself. Still, a promise is a promise.
But I'd feel a lot safer if you were there. Can we come with you?
There's something odd about this invitation, coming to me out of the blue.
I probably should keep an eye on the proceedings as Thor but--
You're right. It would be fun. Don't worry, if there is trouble, I'll--
--I'll shout loudly for the mighty Thor.
Don't be silly! Thor is wonderful, of course. But I'll hardly need him to protect me...

...when you're around!
"When you're around?!?" Ha! How blind these mortals be!
Unless he anticipates a problem...!
Show me the scientist Klaus Voorhees!
And yet... my brother paused.
How unlike the lovesick fool to hesitate to fulfill any request from his beloved Jane.
My moment of triumph is at hand. I stole the universal antivenom formula but I took that fool, the late Dr. Shecktor's notes, on how it was made as well!
No one will question that it is my discovery!
As the masked Cobra, I'll release the poisonous reptiles.
Then--in my scientist persona--I'll charge a fortune to cure those bitten. I'll be rich!
That's it?! The entire purpose of his plan?! How petty is his ambition.
Still it's a start. I can build on it... elaborate!
Thor refuses to forsake the mortal woman. But I will make her abandon Thor...
...and reveal to Odin the fool Thor really is.

THE NEXT DAY...
The lions are cool, Dr. Blake, but I can't wait to see the Reptile and Amphibian House!
Yeah? Why's that?
They have a king cobra. It's the world's most poisonous reptile. And a gila monster. And poison arrow frogs!

They have regular animals, too...but the poisonous ones are the coolest!
You had to ask--

Ooh!
What's wrong?
My...lips! For a second, it felt like a bee stung me.

Don't look so worried, Don. I'm sure it's nothing.
Nothing but a tiny spell!
REPT

Jane Foster's lips will burn to kiss my brother! He, too, will feel their magical allure.
Soon, their lips will meet...and, at that instant, the Prince of Asgard will take the form of whatever animal is nearest!
Though the mortal woman is afraid of snakes, I, personally, am rather hoping for a frog!
Beyond this door is the fully automated control room. It's off-limits to the public.
Behind it is the storeroom where we keep food...
CLICK
CLICK
CLICK
...and traps and netting for when we have to move our more dangerous--
?

SCHWIPPT!
SCHWIPPT!
The Herpetarium doors have opened!
SCHWIPPT!
There's been a malfunction! Everyone, please, walk toward the exits!

This happens just as we pass the enclosures of the world's most venomous creatures! Not a coincidence!

We have to hurry!

It's like a terrible nightmare!

Is it...? Jane, I--

--I need to get you out of here!
The doors are locked!
We're trapped!
EXIT
Go back the way we came in! Head for the entrance!
Why's everybody freaking out? The snakes are probably more scared than they are!
But--aren't scared snakes likelier to bite?
Don? DON!
Jane! Don't fight the crowd. You could fall!
Go on! I'll follow--

--as the *Mighty Thor!*

The villain responsible for this madness will have sealed the main entrance, also...
...but he reckoned without the fury of my hammer Mjolnir!
REPTIL
SHRAK-KOOM!
Dr. Blake's still inside!
Ron, run! Find a guard and tell him what happened.
I have to go back inside and find the doctor. He...he might need me.
This is priceless! The mortal woman-- imperiling herself to save the Mighty Thor...
...unaware that her very lips will seal his doom! Priceless!

Someone opened those cages...
...and since the controls are fully automated...
CONTROL ROOM
...the override command must have come from the control room!
BWOOM!

Don! D-Don!
This is where he fell... I think!
Omigosh, a cobra!
This is awful! And I don't see Don anywhere!

Is that... Thor? If the control room door's open, maybe Don's inside.

COBRA!
Irradiated venom has made me fast, Thunder god--
--and the venomous darts of the Cobra may prove fatal... even to you!
Unlikely!
In any case, they'll not get close enough to strike me.
PTHIPP
PTHKK
PTHTHIP
PTHHIP

Don? Don, are you in there--?
The answer to that is yes... and no!

Now get into the Cobra's arms so Thor can rescue you!
Ooph!

Jane!
EXIT
You know this woman? Excellent! Because she's now my hostage!
Keep back... and no one will get hurt!

What are you waiting for, brother? Where's your backbone?
Play the hero, since you're so good at it!

Save the girl...and earn Loki's special kiss!
Thor! H-help!

Patience, my darling. In a moment, the Cobra will cease to be a menace!
Keep back, Thunder god!
W- where are you taking me?

There's a storage room in back--!
Storage room--?
With equipment for handling the reptiles, you silly woman! And food-- live rats and bugs--for the animals.
More importantly, there's a staff exit into the park. And beyond that, escape... freedom!

You heard him, brother! Look! A convenient croc-net!
What are you waiting for? It's showtime!

If this will hold a crocodile...

...surely it will snare a Cobra!
You'll never catch me that way!

I beg to differ! The creature doth not live that can outrun the Hammer of Thor!
KLOKKK!

I see the Cobra agrees with me.
Ohh. He's not badly hurt, is he?

Now you're worried about the health of that lame villain?
People are coming. You need to kiss my brother before it's too late.
Forget leaving his transformation to chance! No snakes or frogs in the room. Ah! A rat!

The perfect form for the mighty Thor!
He's all right, Jane.
He's just... unconscious, then?
Talk. Talk. Talk! Small wonder Odin still isn't a grandfather!

Kiss the girl, brother, and get it over with!
My hammer just tapped him. Gently.

Very... gently...
That's the way!

...mayhap too gently.
PTHIPP
PTHKK
PTHTHIP
PTHHIP
Jane! Behind me!

Ohhhh...
SMOOCH

...NOOOOO!
What--?! Who?!
Not this! By Odin's beard, anything but this...*
T-thor? D-did you see--?
I thought I saw...?
Saw what, Jane?
WHAP!

I...I'm not sure. I thought... but it can't be.
It must have been a hallucination.
Or maybe I was grazed by one of his poison darts. Or...something...
Come, Jane! 'Tis time to turn the Cobra over to the authorities.
Yeah. Okay. And then I have to...find Don. DON!!
Thor, have you seen Donald Blake?
SSSSSSSSSSSSSSSSSSSSS
I don't believe this! Why do these things always happen to me?!

REPTILES
The boy alerted us that the reptiles were loose, Thor! But we didn't expect anything like this mess!
It's lucky you were around.
Do you need more help?
The zoo-keepers have things under control.
I'm worried about Donald Blake. I don't see him out here!
He's... helping the zoo officials deal with this crisis. He should be with you shortly.
I almost kissed Thor. What's wrong with me? It's Donald Blake that I love.
We almost kissed. Perhaps someday I can tell her who I truly am.

HAHAHAHAHAHA!

ASGARD...

My favored son still moons over the mortal woman. Still, I find it rankles less... for now! She shows some spirit.

Never have I seen Loki so thoroughly snared by one of his own tricks!

And never have I been so greatly amused.

When it pleases me, I will release the trickster...in gratitude for the merriment he has just given me.

But I fear that in my mind that Loki will ever remain the Rat Royale of Ruses!

And once again, a great roa of laughter rings out acros the battlements of Asgard

#8

US AIR FORCE BASE
BOSTON 1945
Our info was on the money-- someone's stealing the new drone plane!
We can't let it reach enemy lines! Go for the ramp, Cap, we can still make it!
Gotcha!
Bucky, I can't reach it! Don't try this alone!
Drop off into the water, lad!
It's okay, Cap, I can--
Wait! I-- I think this bird is booby-tr-
K-SKROOM!
Bucky! Nooooo!!!
"No..."
No...

Captain...?
NO!!
Holy cow, w-we actually did it--
He's alive!
Where am I? Who are you people? Where's Bucky?!
Captain, please try to stay calm...
I am Major Sharon Carter of the Strategic Hazard Intervention Espionage Logistics Directorate. We found you in the Atlantic a month ago. You're among friends...
Lock and load, boys, he looks mad...
"Strategic Hazard"...? Is that what you SS types are calling yourselves now?
If you're looking for a hazard, Fraulein, then this is your lucky day. Pleased to meet you...
The name's
CAPTAIN AMERICA!
Aargh!
Unngh!

Stun-beams only! Don't hurt him!
Don't hurt him?!
SKKOW!
SKKOW!
Ooof!
Hnnngh!
SKKOW!
You goose-steppers need to get out of the lab more often...
...you need the exercise!
This place is a maze--I've never seen an Axis bunker this big!
And those weapons they were using--like something out of H.G. Wells! It won't take them long to find me...
Got to stop using their exits--
K-KRUNCH!
And make one of my own!
Why can't I remember where I was before they caught me? What's happened to Bucky?
Straighten up, Rogers--deal with that later. I could be heading for the fight of my life...
I'm probably in the heart of...
Berlin...?

TIMES SQUARE, NEW YORK. TODAY
Rock till you puke! Rock till you puke! Rock till you puke!!!
More bad news from Wall Street as banking giant Richmond & Royle collapses...
...global warming-related disaster in The Philippines...
CUP A RICE

Don't miss the premiere of Hot Mods & Jerk Nerds, this Thursday on the Babel Channel!
THE LEGEND REBORN!
SCOTT GRAY-WRITER
CRAIG ROUSSEAU-ARTIST
CHRIS SOTOMAYOR-COLORIST
DAVE SHARPE-LETTERS
HENRY et GURU-COVER
PAUL ACERIOS-PRODUCTION
RALPH MACCHIO-CONSULTING
NATHAN COSBY-EDITOR
JOE QUESADA-EDITOR IN CHIEF
DAN BUCKLEY-PUBLISHER
The new Kamasuki GT-1000--the latest model from Japan...
車
THE REALLY LATE SHOW
ROY'S FAMOUS PIZZA
WACKDONALD'S
SOUP
BAGELS
ATM

Get off the road, flag-boy!
HONK! HONK! HONK! HONK! HONK! HONK!
It can't be...I must be dreaming...
Hey, move yer star-spangled tail, you whacko!

Whoa. There's a guy in need of some serious therapy...
Hey, that's a *buck-and-a-half*, pal!
A dollar-fifty... for a *news-paper*...?
DAILY TI
THE VOICE
And the *date*... the date is...
2009...?

Hey...dude... are you *okay?* You look majorly *freaked*.
I don't want to bum you out, but Independence Day is weeks away...
Wh-what...?
Bucky!
Ah, no... *Rick Jones.* Have guitar, will travel...
I'm available for kids' shows, bar mitzvahs and *costume parties,* which I'm guessing is where you're headed...
Sorry. For a second I thought...but no. I *remember* now.
Bucky's *gone.*
Everyone I ever cared for... they must *all* be gone. I'm *alone*...
...stranded in *the future.*

He found a way into the subway system, Major Carter--that's a lot of ground to cover.
He could have surfaced anywhere...
Don't give me excuses, Palmer!
Rogers is dressed up like the Fourth of July, he's not going to be hard to spot!
We'd better find him fast, Sharon...
What do you mean, Sid?
The only way to wake Cap up was to accelerate his metabolic functions...
If he doesn't get a stabilizer shot of vita-serum within the hour, his body will burn up...and we'll be minus one living legend.
Forever.
Oh, great! I want every New York field agent on this! Find Captain America!
Mason! Get that vita-serum shot ready!
Yes, Dr. Levine...
Mason to Horde Leader: the target is loose.
Hail Hydra...
So...you're Captain America, huh? The real Captain America? Sentinel of Liberty, Spirit of '76, Mr. Apple Pie... that guy?
I guess that must sound absurd to you.
Well, my mind's as open as the next guy's, but that is one big hero sandwich to swallow, dude!
I'd better humor the poor guy...
So...uh... how come you're not, like, a hundred years old by now?
I've been trying to work that out myself. Maybe it has something to do with the way it all started...

"Times were pretty tough when I was a boy. New York was hit hard by the Depression. We didn't have a lot, but what you had, you shared...
"By 1940, the Axis powers were stampeding across Europe. I knew America would be next on their list...
"So I tried to join up. No good. Skinny Steve Rogers was judged too frail for the army...
"But I was given a chance to become a test subject...of The Super-Soldier Project.
"A brilliant scientist, Abraham Erskine, had devised a way to increase a man's physique. It sounded insane...
"But when the wave of energy flooded through me...when I felt my muscles expand...
"...I knew I would never be the same again.
"The plan was to create an entire army of Super-Soldiers, but Dr. Erskine was captured by a spy soon after. His secrets died went with him.

"So they turned me into something else--a symbol for the Allied Forces to rally around...
"I became Captain America.
"I didn't fight alone, of course. I had the best partner a soldier could ever hope for--James Buchanan Barnes. The world knew him as Bucky.
"We tackled every monster the enemy could throw at us including the worst of them all--The Red Skull.
"We knew we had the Skull and all his ilk on the ropes--the war was almost done. Soon we'd have a chance to rest...
"But that day never came.
"Did the Super-Soldier treatment preserve me somehow? Slow my heart-beat? Slow my aging?
"Maybe I'll never know for sure. But here I am."

Hey, you...uh, just told me your secret identity, dude...
What does it matter now? This is a different age--and one I don't like the look of. All I see is madness and trivia and... wantonness!
Great Day in the Morning, those girls are barely dressed!
Waaaait a minute, pal! Sure, there's a ton of dumb stuff floating through the ether, but some-times you need a little distraction--times are getting tough again, y'know!
You may not like it, but America's ditching a lotta old-school thinking--we're finally starting to look ahead!
All I am is "old-school."
Maybe you're right, Rick. Maybe I shouldn't judge. But my war is long over.
What use am I to America now?
SKRAZZ
SKRAZZ
SKRAZZ
Back away, citizens! Make way...
Eeeeeeee!
K-THOOM!
Aahhhh!
...for the Hordes of Hydra!
Captain America! Welcome to the 21st Century! We have no desire to harm you...
Accept us as your friends and surrender now!

You know, I may be new to this time...and not up on current events just yet...
Whoa!
...but I know a nest of rats when I see one!
Aargh!
KLANNG!
Get him, you idiots! He's just one man!
Yaaah!
THWOK!
SHWAK!
Aooow!
Hnnngh!
SKRAK!
I've got his shield!
That's mighty kind of you, fella! Let me take it off your hands!
WHAMM!
Aaaah!
I'm gonna give you goons a piece of advice...
SKRAZZ

...the next time you take to the air, put the pilot in a cockpit!
Nynngh!
No!!!
FWOKK!
Last stop, gents: ground floor!
Look out!
Aaaaah!
KA-THRAAM!
Who is that guy?!
He's gorgeous!
This is beyond awesome...
I'll be asking some questions in a minute--I hope you boys are the talkative type...
THWAKK!
...otherwise I may lose my temper!
Use the Neuro-Wave, fool! Hurry!

The Neuro-Wave paralyzes any living thing in its path, Captain...
Nnnnghh!
ZREEEEEEE
I am shielded from its effects but you are not so fortunate!
As I said, I have no wish to harm you. In fact, this vita-serum will calm your raging body and save your life...
You'll be a very useful tool for Hydra once you've been re-educated...
You know who we are, don't you, Captain? Our name has changed... our uniforms are new...
...but you know who we are.

Our Supreme Leader is looking forward to seeing you... Let's not keep him waiting...
FWANNNNG!
Eh?
Sorry to interrupt, dude-- thought I'd play your bud here a little lullaby!

Uhhh...
Much obliged, Rick.
You and I are going to talk some more, mister...
...after you wake up!
SHWOK!
AAAAAKK!

Maybe I should thank you. I wasn't sure what I could offer this new century...
But now I know. As long as there's scum like you still roaming the world--men who freely destroy and terrorize to achieve their aims...
Men who seek to crush the ideals that this country holds dear...
Then my war is not over!

Wa-hooo! Go, Cap!
You tell 'em, man!
Wow! I mean... WOW!
Is that really Captain America?
Yeah... I think it is...

Ughhh...
Cap! What's wrong?!

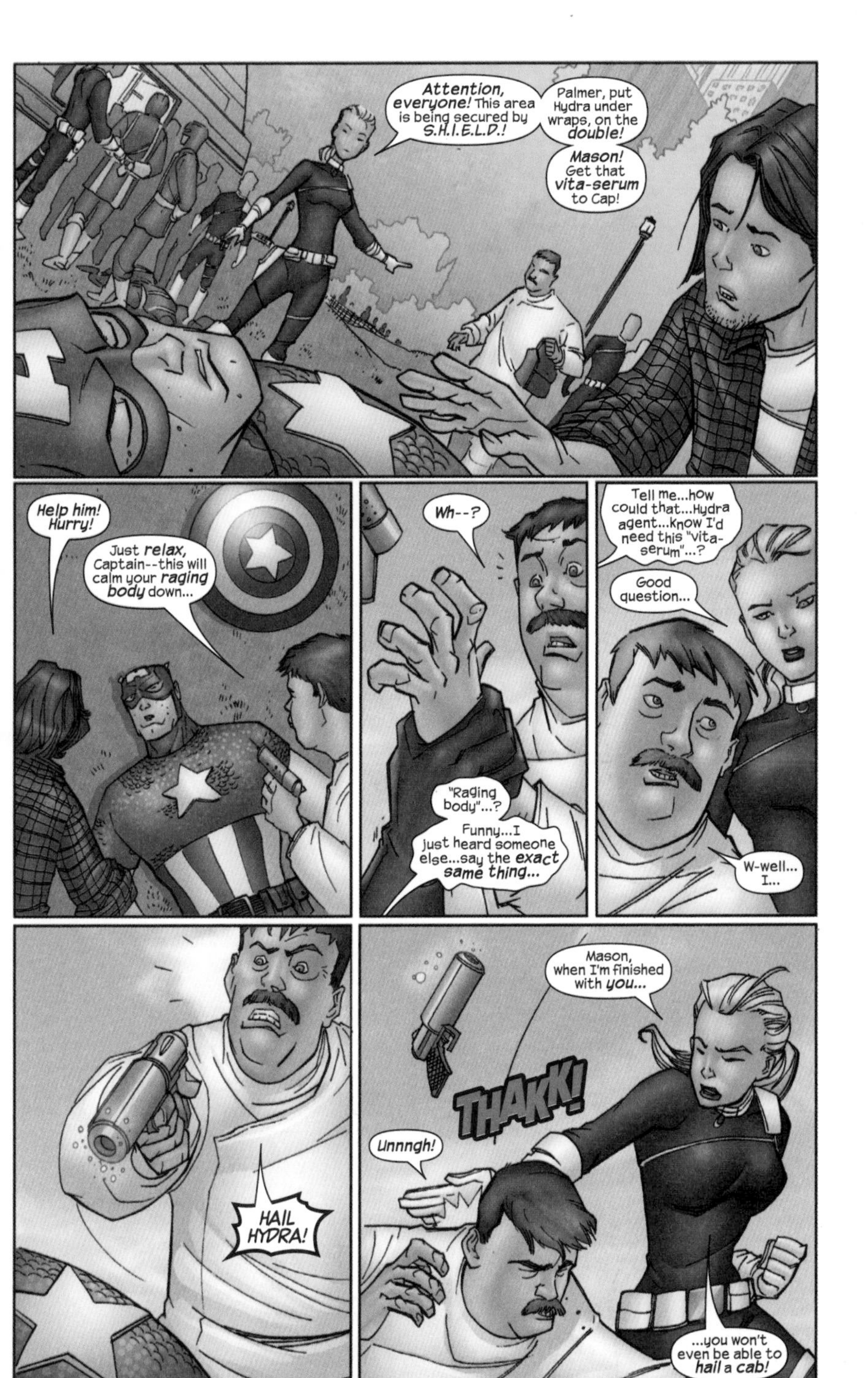
Attention, everyone! This area is being secured by S.H.I.E.L.D.!
Palmer, put Hydra under wraps, on the double!
Mason! Get that vita-serum to Cap!
Help him! Hurry!
Just relax, Captain--this will calm your raging body down...
Wh--?
"Raging body"...?
Funny...I just heard someone else...say the exact same thing...
Tell me...how could that...Hydra agent...know I'd need this "vita-serum"...?
Good question...
W-well... I...
HAIL HYDRA!
Mason, when I'm finished with you...
THAKK!
Unnngh!
...you won't even be able to hail a cab!

THE NEXT DAY...
So you've checked out okay, Cap?
Fit and fine, Rick. These S.H.I.E.L.D. guys know their onions...
Well, we "guys" do our best, Captain...
Major Carter! I want to apologize for my behavior yesterday--
Forget it. Like you said-- we needed the exercise...
You've got a lot of catching up to do, Captain. I've assigned a historian to bring you up to speed and act as your liaison. You can start today if you'd--
No thank you, Major.
I don't want to learn about my country from lectures-- I plan to discover it first-hand. I'll agree to a liaison, but I want it to be a man on the street...
What do you say, Rick?
Wha--?
It isn't just Captain America who needs to find his way in a new world...
Steve Rogers has to do the same.
C'mon, Rick... let's go see America.
I'm all for that, dude. What say we start at a steak house? I'm starving!
THE BEGINNING!

1942!
...these papers were stolen from the research department of one of our most important weapons manufacturers.
We need them back at all costs! The war effort depends upon it!
The thief is a carpenter, currently employed in Hollywood building film sets.
You are to go undercover and get the papers back before he has a chance to hand them over to the enemy. Understood?
Sir.
This file should tell you all you need to know. You are instructed to leave right away... we'll square things with your unit.
Time is of the essence.
Thank you, sir.
"Karl Foeppl," eh? Well, Herr Foeppl...
FOEPPL, KARL
...you just messed with the wrong country!
CAPTAIN AMERICA
in: SPY FOR THE CAMERAS!
Story ROGER LANGRIDGE
Art CRAIG ROUSSEAU
Color CHRIS SOTOMAYOR
Letters DAVE SHARPE
Consulting RALPH MACCHIO
Editor NATHAN COSBY
Editor in Chief JOE QUESADA
Publisher DAN BUCKLEY

TWO DAYS LATER...
HOLLYWOODLAND
DEMOCRATIC STUDIOS
Rogers! Rogers!!
Get over here, Rogers! You may be the worst blasted actor I've ever laid my sorry eye on, but we need another extra in this scene and we're paying you fifty cents an hour!
SALOON
Yessir!
I swear I don't know where they find people like you! Shouldn't you be in the army, anyhow?
Flat feet, sir. And speaking of the army...
...you wouldn't happen to be related to a guy called Duffy, would you?
My family tree is none of your confounded business! Hit your mark, you boob!!
Right you are, Sarge... er, sir!
Oof!
Ow!
Can't you look where you're going, you dimpled clod?
I'm awfully sorry, Miss. You just started in make-up this morning, right? "Roz," was it?
"Rosalind" to my friends. "Miss Hepburn" to you, Dimples.
Aagh! Now I've lost him, thanks to you! Where the heck...?

Oh, never mind! He can't have gone far!
Hmmm...

Hey, chum. Ever wanted to be in a cowboy picture?
Why, uh...er...
Swell. Put this on and stand on set over there, will you?
Good man.

Aha! There you are, you strange little fellow!
Karl Foeppl! At last!

Huh? Where'd he go?

CREEEAK
What th--

AAAAAHHHH!

OOOFF!
WHUMMMP
Are you all right, Miss--?
Never mind me! Get that no-good rat!

Foeppl! Stop! You're only making this harder for yourself!
Hah! So you say, Amerikaner pig!
puff puff Jiminy Whillikers! pant Those boys... can sure...puff run! But if I don't...get some pictures...the chief will have my press pass!
For the Fatherland! For the Führer!
SPANNNGGG
Aaghh!!
Still...time... to capture his liaison...
Gehen Sie! Schnell! Schnell!
AAAHH!
Smile!
PFAFF
Oops.

LATER...
I found another one! I'm pretty sure that's the last of them.
Swell.
So everything's fine now! You got your papers, Karl What's-his-name is in the clink. Don't I get a little "thank you"?
Of course, Miss Hepburn. Thank you for collecting the papers. Thank you for risking your neck.
Thank you for getting in my way. Thank you for letting the other spy escape...
Oh! I got in your way, did I? Did it ever occur to you that you completely ruined my undercover exposé?
How? By saving your life?

Listen, buster! We reporters represent freedom of information! Isn't freedom what this silly war is all about?
Reporters... you're all alike! You confuse freedom with the right to endanger yourselves and others.
If you really want to help the war effort, I'm sure there's plenty of sewing that needs doing...

Why, you... you're... you're...

sigh... gorgeous.

"Most great men and women are not perfectly rounded in their personalities, but are instead people whose one driving enthusiasm is so great it makes their faults seem insignificant."
--Charles A. Cerami

THE END